MW01105294

Some young reviewers who have enjoyed books such as:
Pilgrim's Progress, Chronicles of Narnia, Artemis Fowl, Kingdom's Dawn, Grayfox, Across Five Aprils, Indian in the Cupboard, Raising Dragons, the Hardy Boys series, the City of Ember series, etc...

Had this to say about Light for the Sacra Vellum...

Excellent book! Great analogy! Pulls you right in! Can't wait for the next one!
Courtney Flonta (12 years old. Chesapeake, Virginia)

I liked the book a lot because it had a good and clear message. I can't wait to read the sequel to find out what happens to the citizens of Graceville.
Jesse Johnson (12 years old. Somerset, New Jersey)

I was practically holding my breath when I wondered what would happen to TW's Sacra Vellum... I can't wait to read the sequel
Christopher Aboagye (11 years old. Gaithersburg, Maryland)

I thought the book was funny in the beginning, but when it got to the middle it became intense. I understood the concept totally and I can't wait to see what will happen next.
Adeyoola Adeniji (11 years old. Tampa, Florida)

It reminded me of *Pilgrim's Progress*. I can't wait to read the sequel!
Rachel Epp (10 years old. North Carolina)

This book is really good! I love the legends in the story. They make it very interesting. I'm so glad there will be a sequel. I think my mom and dad would enjoy reading it too. Two thumbs up!
Benjamin Campbell (10 years old. Chesapeake, Virginia)

LIGHT FOR THE SACRA VELLUM

Cathy O. Idowu

Illustrated by
Lisa Wright

RiteQuest
www.ritequest.com

The Graceville Chronicles

Light for the Sacra Vellum

ISBN: 978-0-9801484-0-4

For more information, contact RiteQuest Books at info@ritequest.com

Author: Catherine O. Idowu
Illustrator: Lisa Wright
Edited and proofread by:
Emily Wright, Lisa Epp, and Elaine Dudley

First Printing—January 2008
Printed in the USA

Dedication

To the Lord God—
By whose grace this has been made possible.

GRACEVILLE

Prologue

"Come over here quickly!" the Chief Townsitter hastily beckoned Cheerlos, the Tempostry-help. The Chief was bent over the Sacra Vellum, holding an almost blinding light over one of its pages. He turned his head, looked into the face of the Tempostry-help, and beamed, "Do you see it?"

"See what?" asked the perplexed helper who had only come into the room to gather up the empty teacups, a nightly ritual at the Tempostry.

"The words. I'm beginning to pick up words from the Sacra Vellum. See. Read this."

Cheerlos narrowed his eyes to sharpen his focus and lowered his head until his nose almost touched the page. "Sir, I think a spider got trapped between your pages when you last shut your Sacra Vellum. What I see is an impression of a pressed spider from the previous page. It's neither a word, nor even a letter." He straightened, packed up the teacups, and left the room silently.

The Chief Townsitter, embarrassed from yet another fruitless attempt at reading the Sacra Vellum, sighed and sat back into his chair. It was eleven minutes after 10 o'clock. The light-makers at Powers-on-the-Hill had convinced him that nothing could be hidden from the piercing strength of their latest lamp. This was the thirteenth lamp he had purchased from them this year in his attempt to read the words of the Sacra Vellum. He suddenly got up and angrily marched out of his room into the dimly lit narrow hallway yelling, "Has anyone read the Sacra Vellum tonight?" There were a dozen rooms on both sides of the hallway, a Townsitter occupying each. Their daily work at the Tempostry was to sit, meditate, and attempt to read the Sacra Vellum. There could have been a response offered from any of the eleven other

rooms, but none came. He continued, "We know that the great commander of the whole earth, Imortul, has chosen the people of Graceville to be the most precious people to him in the entire Monkonian region. He has told us that the secrets of life and joy are within the pages of the Sacra Vellum which he handed down to us. Yet no Townsitter, no Graceville citizen, absolutely nobody is able to read the pages of this book! Why he decreed that the book must be read at 10 o'clock at night, I do not know. There is no light bright enough to reveal the pages at that nor at any other time!" His anger had given momentum to his feet, and he charged back and forth the hallway, ranting on, "It should not surprise us that we are constantly mocked by all the neighboring towns of the Monkonian mountain: Powers-on-the-Hill, Angertown, Selfville, Feathersburg, and other little hamlets. They say to us, 'Your Sacra Vellum has brought you nothing, yet you foolishly hold on to it. We at least have some measure of pleasure.'" He paused again and waited for a response. His heavy breathing was the only sound. No one seemed to have been provoked by his passionate discourse. "Shouldn't this have provoked them?" was his astonished thought. He crept to a door that was slightly open. He peeped through. The large, barrel-bodied Townsitter was fast asleep, snoring terribly loudly,

with an opened Sacra Vellum bobbing on his heaving chest. He peeped through another. This Townsitter, rocking back and forth in a squeaky rocking chair, stared wide-eyed at the wall straight ahead of him.

"What are you doing?" asked the Chief.

"Just staring at the wall," the obviously uninterested Townsitter answered lazily.

"But the wall is blank," the Chief Townsitter expressed a puzzled look at his choice of an evening past-time.

"So is the Sacra Vellum," his cynical answer came with a loud yawn, further confirming his lack of interest in dialoging with the Chief.

Disappointed that no one was up for a debate, the Chief Townsitter restlessly retired to his room. "What was the benefit of their pitiful existence?" he wondered to himself as he settled into his bed. They spent endless days, sitting in their rooms, hoping for the revelation of the Sacra Vellum. Such a lifestyle of much inactivity had caused the Townsitters to be stocky and wide-bellied in stature. They also had very little dealings with their own people. Their reason for having minimal interaction was that they were often in lengthy periods of meditation and reflection. But some wondered if it was not due to the awkwardness of being unable to read the Sacra Vellum. Yes, Imortul had given them additional responsibilities such as providing justice for the poor and the needy, but they couldn't be bothered with such "inconveniences." The people would have to manage on their own.

Cheerlos stuck his head through the doorway. "I'm done for the night, sir. Goodnight."

The Chief Townsitter finally found an opportunity to engage someone in discussion. "Before you go, did you hear any of what I had said in the hallway?"

"Some of it, sir; I do know you were rather angry at your failed reading, but, sir, I have some ideas."

"What ideas, Cheerlos?" asked the Chief Townsitter as he attempted to cover himself with his blanket.

"Well, sir, everyone thinks that Graceville is a contrary society of very peculiar people. While it is a thing of pride that our Sacra Vellum sets us apart, every one of us is frustrated that we are unable to fulfill the decree given by Imortul. Perhaps you might consider adopting some of the customs of the other Monkonian towns," Cheerlos somewhat hesitantly suggested.

"What would those be?" inquired the Chief Townsitter.

"For one, they are ruled by Lords and Lady Lords and are not depending on words from any book to bring them happiness. Instead, they have a temple. It is built of gold on one of the highest peaks of the mountains and is dedicated to Mee. Everything they do, buy, or sell is all done for Mee. Mee is worshipped in whatever way each person decides they want to worship. As a result, they constantly provide themselves with momentary pleasures to stay happy. Not so in Graceville. Our town is full of confused citizens, burdened mothers, grumpy fathers, and children with unhappy faces."

"Are you suggesting that escaping from the reality of our present failures will provide us with permanent happiness? You are so foolish. If you were not a Tempostry-help, you would have no other job. How can you suggest that we leave our dedication to the pre-eminence and seek after figments of our imagination? Indeed, Graceville will remain, in your own words, 'a contrary society of very peculiar people.' Graceville will continue to be overseen by the Townsitters on Imortul's behalf as we continue to scrupulously preserve the Sacra Vellum." The Chief Townsitters's voice bellowed at a now startled Cheerlos.

"Yes, sir, I'd better take my leave," Cheerlos submitted as he backed out of the room.

"Cheerlos, one more thing...ring the Tempostry Bell. It is time we nurture a new Townsitter for the coming generation and preserve our future from wayward ideas like yours."

"Yes, sir, I will do just that." He quietly shut the Chief Townsitter's door and quickly made his way toward the Tempostry Bell.

1

The cry of the newborn child filled the air. A tired smile broke across Eyrene's face as she looked expectantly at the midwife who was inspecting the new child.

"It's a boy," the midwife announced rather flatly, quite a contrast to the joyful event that had just occurred. She had delivered hundreds of babies, so this birth seemed to hold no thrill for her. The tired mother was beaming with joy, paying no attention to the bell that chimed in the distance. The echoing sound was coming from the Tempostry. It continued to chime for another five minutes.

"There goes the bell!" announced the midwife, whose eyes had widened with sudden excitement. "Do you hear it? A significant thing has just occurred. You have just given birth to our next Townsitter!" This time she broke into a smile, revealing a hint of pitilessness. "You have two years to nurse him, and then you must turn him over to the Tempostry where they will raise him to become one of the servants of Imortul."

Upon hearing these words, the new mother shot up into a sitting position on the birthing bed, her body suddenly strengthened as one ready for a fight. "No, he will not!" she responded in confident defiance. "My son will not be shut up in the Tempostry for the rest of his life. He shall be like every other boy. He shall grow up to play hide and seek with his father, run around the square with his friends, enjoy his dreams, and grow up to become a wonderful citizen, just like his father..."

"But, Eyrene," the midwife firmly interrupted as she swaddled the newborn boy in a clean, white cotton blanket and handed him to his protective mother, "Your son was born at the time of the chiming. You know our traditions. We have no Lords and Lady Lords. Imortul is our only commander, and he has appointed Townsitters to care for us on his behalf. You know very well that Townsitters do not just drop from the sky, young woman. Our tradition says that the first male to be born around the chiming of the Tempostry Bell is to be made a Townsitter. I am not saying anything strange to you. Now we must stain his right toe with charcoal dust and seal him for Imortul's noble service." She paused for a second. "Clarisse!" she screeched for her assisting nurse who had just stepped outside to inform the waiting young father of the safe delivery of his baby boy. "Bring the charcoal dust, we have a new Townsitter. I must stain him before the mother nurses him."

"No! No! No!" screamed a terrified Eyrene.

But the midwife fiercely interrupted, this time shouting, "You are not the only mother who has had to give up her son to the Tempostry! You should be glad that your family has been called to such a noble sacrifice for the service of Imortul."

"What service?" Eryene bravely shouted back. "How can Imortul be pleased that the men, called to show our people care, are hidden away in a Tempostry, while the people on the streets are mad, sad, and bad?" She took a sharp, deep breath. She was sweating profusely, the four bright lamps around her only making it worse. She thought of her husband on the other side of the birthing room wall. He had no idea of what was going on. She was determined not to lose her son to the lifestyle of the Townsitters. "My son is not going to be one of them. There is more for my son's life than being adorned in elaborate robes and headwear. I'm convinced Imortul can have a different plan for this servant." She pulled her swaddled son closer to her and looked at his peaceful sleeping face. Long black eyelashes, a tiny snub nose and delicately pursed lips were perfectly arranged on his beautiful skin. "No! It's not going to happen," she fiercely insisted.

Then it dawned on her that Clarisse would be back any minute with the charcoal dust. Her son's fate would be sealed! "Aw! Aw!" she moaned, laying her swaddled son on the bed beside her. Then she doubled over and continued to scream, "Aghhhhhhh! Aghhhhh!"

"What is it?" asked the now-confused midwife in a panicked voice.

"I have a terrible pain in my stomach. Help me! Please get me some tonic," she whispered between what seemed to be painful, short breaths. She appeared to suffer from a stomachache and wheezing all rolled into one.

"You have just had a baby, and you should not have agitated yourself in such a manner. Now there's no telling what is wrong with you," the midwife said as she rushed out of the room to rummage through the medicine chest for tonic.

Here was Eryene's only chance. She jumped off the bed, grabbed her son, and dashed out of the birthing house into the cobbled street. She was thankful that it was a cloudy night. "Asher!" she shouted for her husband who was leaning against the outside wall, still waiting to be called in to see his new son. Asher rushed to her side.

"What's going on, my dear?" he asked in a panicked whisper.

"No time to talk, Asher," she panted heavily. "The midwife and the Townsitters will be after us anytime now."

"What's going on?" Asher questioned, extremely puzzled. "Has he been named a Townsitter?" he gasped, searching Eyrene's frantic expression for clues, as he attempted to piece everything together.

"No, his toe has not been stained yet. He's still ours. Here, you carry the boy." She pushed the swaddled child into his arms.

Asher couldn't help but momentarily stop and gaze at his newborn son. "Perfect features! Look at his head, all bald except for this little black curly tuft upon his tiny forehead. Perhaps this is a sign from Imortul that he will be a ray of hope in the midst of surrounding emptiness," he thought aloud. Then he paused briefly, watching his peacefully sleeping son within in arms. "I name him TW."

"Asher! I hear footsteps," Eryene fervently whispered. With violent urgency she gathered the hem of her skirt in her hands and started to run down the street. Asher quickly caught up with her, his prized bundle secure in the crook of his arm.

"I know this is urgent, Eryene, but stay calm. I will get us out of town tonight. First, we've got to run home and gather some bread, clothing, and blankets. Most importantly, we must take our Sacra Vellum with us."

"Oh, our readerless book," muttered Eyrene, trying not to sound too sarcastic. She wasn't sure of the point in taking a book that they would probably never read. It seemed just an extra burden right now.

"You must not talk like that, Eyrene," said Asher, almost sternly. "We have hope that we will someday read our precious book. If not us, our wonderful son may. He will not be groping around in some dark Tempostry, creating strange ideas on how Imortul would desire us to live. Someday he will read the Sacra Vellum and understand the ways of Imortul."

Suddenly interrupting her husband, Eyrene fiercely interjected, "Asher, if that's to happen, we've got to run!"

12 years later...

2

"Professor Chops Up Pages of the Sacra Vellum for Confetti at Daughter's Wedding." The unthinkable incident was splashed across the front page of the *Graceville Times*. The *Times* quoted the professor as saying, "I find it absolutely ridiculous that I own a book that I cannot read. Confetti was a better use for it." All of Graceville was talking about the outrageous event. It also brought back memories of an equally provocative episode that had happened twelve years earlier. It was said that a young couple had brazenly defied the sacred customs of the Townsitters, and had escaped from Graceville, taking with them their newborn Townsitter.

This recent incident released a torrent of frustration that had been building up over many years: what were they going to do about their inability to read the Sacra Vellum? It was clearly established that the Sacra Vellum would now become whatever people wished it to be.

Attitudah, the flamboyant florist, came up with her own useful idea for the Sacra Vellum. She placed a large basket outside her flower shop, loudly inviting people to contribute their Sacra Vellum in exchange for some money. Being a talented designer, she quickly invented a variety of exotic floral decorations from the donated books. She callously ripped the leather covers off each Sacra Vellum to separate the hundreds of pages within them, dyed the sheets into various floral colors, and then shaped them into what she aptly named "petal papyrus." Each book yielded hundreds of petals.

Attitudah, admiring her handiwork, called out to her orphaned nephew, TW, "I've found good use for your time after school, young boy." She carefully arranged her delicate handiwork in a clean wheelbarrow inside her shop. "Each day after school you will take this wheelbarrow and peddle the petals in the marketplace." TW's stomach sank, and tears welled up in his eyes upon hearing his aunt's firm command. "It'll keep you out of mischief and get you a little allowance too," she reasoned further, caring nothing for his show of emotion.

Life in the marketplace was absolutely humiliating for TW. The agony of sitting in the open market place in full view of all passers-by was torture to him. Aunty Attitudah had insisted that he park the wheelbarrow right at the entry-arch of the market. He could not be missed. The spot was paying off for his aunt, but for him, he was losing everything: friends, confidence, happiness. The Sacra Vellum held so much meaning to him, especially because it was the only inheritance he had received from his parents. His thoughts would often wander to his time as a younger boy. His parents would sit him between them every night at 10 o'clock, waiting and hoping for the day they would be able to read the Sacra Vellum. His father would caress young TW's hair saying, "Someday, son. Someday we shall see."

But right now all TW saw were petals. Lots of them! He was so far away from the hope that had been passed down to him. He couldn't even bring himself to say Petal

APOTHECARY
Teas
Sacra Lanterns

Papyrus. He just called them the P's. If someone ordered yellow spotted violet petal papyrus, he'd just make a mental note of ysvp's. It was more bearable that way. "Less mental torture," he thought.

"Hey, TW!"

He was jolted back into reality. He knew that voice. It was the hatmaker. Business had been thriving for him since he started trimming ladies' hats with the petals. His eyes quickly darted back and forth to see if any of his schoolmates would witness the shameful sale that was about to occur. This had become his natural reaction every time his name was called at the marketplace.

"Would you tell your aunt I need more of the purple periwinkle petal papyrus?" the hatmaker requested.

"Yes, sir," TW whispered quickly. As immersed as he was in all the Sacra Vellum trading, he did his best to appear aloof from it all. Perhaps his friends would come to understand that he wasn't doing it because he wanted to, but rather because he was forced into it.

Inventions using the Sacra Vellum seemed to be all over the marketplace. TW regretted that he had to be lumped with these Sacra Vellum offenders. Right behind him were the Opportunas. They seemed to be a permanent fixture in the marketplace. Before the booming business of Sacra Vellum wares, they had an eyeball cleaning business, and they also made some additional income reading palms. But now they had jumped on the Sacra Vellum bandwagon.

Pa Opportuna ran a kiosk touting the magical energy of his Sacra lanterns. Just like TW's aunt, he had peeled off the leaves of the Sacra Vellum, dyed them, and used them for lantern shades. He had lanterns of every color hanging all over his kiosk. He claimed that each color radiated a different power. He also burned incense around his kiosk which irritated TW's nostrils, so that he constantly sniffed. Pa always had a long line of customers from Selfville and other surrounding towns. Through the billowing smoke of incense he would give two-minute talks on the restorative powers of the Sacra lanterns.

"For instance," he would say as he walked up and down the line of waiting customers, "if you buy this lilac lantern, it will filter out the dark energies of conflict in your home and begin to release the light of peace. All it takes is thirty days to see your home transformed into a marvelous abode of peace." Money pouches would promptly be opened by over-eager customers. Within minutes, scores of lanterns would be paid for and whipped from the kiosk's shelves. Pa Opportuna always seemed to have a knack for knowing which lantern would suit each customer. If an elderly lady stopped by, for example, he'd be talking about the amber lanterns that absorbed frailty and released youthful energy around the home.

And then there was his wife next door, Ma Opportuna. She ran another despicable kiosk: The Sacra Eternal Teas. "My tea leaves heal every kind of ailment. The tea is contained in the magical sacra sachets so that when it is brewed, healing powers are released right into your teacup," she would tell her long line of mainly out-of-town prospective customers. Then in a loud, cracked voice she would shout into the street, "Come to me with your toe-nail fungus, your boils, and your twitching eyeballs! I have the perfect healing brew for you."

This was all torture to the ears of TW who sat miserably in front of her kiosk, exactly where his aunt had stationed him. Why did he have to sit so close to these deceivers? Didn't he see Ma Opportuna come each day with huge bowls of regular mint tea leaves to bag into the Sacra sachets? How did they suddenly become this magical potion just because she, quite tragically, wrapped them up in paper belonging to his most beloved book?

All he could do in the midst of this whirlwind of deceit was blankly stare at all Pa Opportuna's salivary droppings halfway across the street. Pa Opportuna had a very strange habit of walking away from his kiosk up to the center of the street and emptying his mouth of strange brown grounds. He would do this at least four times each hour until sunset. They actually looked like bird droppings once the sun baked them into the cobblestone. TW also watched to see if any passer-by would accidentally step on them or suddenly notice the brown heaps and dart in one direction or another to avoid them. Observing the little bit of gymnastics from passers-by was a slightly entertaining way to pass the time between papyrus customers, but it couldn't take his mind off the pain of his seeming hopelessness. He had not always been so resigned.

3

For a moment, TW had a flashback to his first week in the marketplace. He, as usual, had been terribly vexed to see Sacra Vellum wares filling the marketplace, especially the deceptive trade of the Opportunas. Righteous indignation filled him. He had thought to himself, "If I sit here and do nothing, this scandalous trade will only continue. It will continue until Graceville is completely emptied of all the Sacra Vellums, including mine." For now, he was comforted knowing his precious book was securely hidden in the roof above the kitchen, but what about all these others being wasted daily in the marketplace? He decided to take on the personal crusade of restoring Graceville's fading glory. He was not going to be just a kid, pacified with lollipops. He had a brave heart and hopefully would come up with a really smart plan to restore the Sacra Vellum.

On the day he was to execute his brilliant plan, he parked his wheelbarrow in front of Ma Opportuna's kiosk as usual. Known to him alone, everything else about that day was to be quite unusual. He was so sure that by the time he was done carrying out his carefully-crafted plan, the Opportunas' deception would be exposed. The Townsitters would call for all Sacra Vellum trade to immediately cease and in recognition of his outstanding bravery at disrupting the Sacra Vellum trade, he would receive a huge reward. More importantly, he would become his school's hero, and win the friendships of his schoolmates afresh.

It was a Saturday, right around noon, the busiest market hour in the week. The lines of customers leading to the Opportuna kiosks seemed endless. The moment was right. This was the perfect stage for his act:

"Aghhhhh! Aghhhhhhh!" He let out a piercing yell,

doubled over, and threw himself on the floor. The lines at the Opportunas' right behind him immediately dispersed, with sympathetic customers rushing to his aid.

"What's wrong, poor child?" a frail, old lady asked.

"Aghh! Aw! Aw! Aw! My stomach," TW continued to wail in a very agitated manner. He even managed to force out a few tears. Several young men picked him up and, to his horror, laid him in the center of the street, right on top of Pa Opportuna's disgusting mouth droppings, which they had hardly noticed because of the seeming emergency. Someone was fanning him. He was sweating from the crowd around him.

"Bring him over here!" Ma Opportuna beckoned the assisting customers. "My tea is going to cure him right before your eyes." That was exactly what TW had hoped she would claim. His plan seemed to be working so far. He was brought in and laid on the cold bare floor of Ma Opportuna's kiosk. She filled a mug with at least twenty ounces of hot brewed tea. "Drink for me, darlin'," she coaxed, baring her orangey-brown, mosaic-looking teeth in a smile of encouragement. This looked like a great marketing moment for her after all. It was her opportunity to prove the healing properties of her tea.

TW took a sip...nasty! Now his stomach really

churned. He was determined to keep his fake ache going for as long as he needed to, until the people would realize that the deceptive potion really didn't work. Then word would spread that the teas were fake.

"Aw! Aw! Aghhh!" he doubled over again, writhing. This time Pa Opportuna ran in from his neighboring kiosk with some foul smelling incense. "Nasty drink! Nasty smell!" TW cringed inwardly. But he had a job to do, and he'd have to tough it out. He was putting himself through a lot to end all this deception.

"Drink some more, son," encouraged Ma Opportuna. How sweet she sounded. But it had to be because she was concerned about her tea sales with customers looking on and waiting for proof. His determination doubled, and he drank some more of the sacra tea.

Pa Opportuna waved his smelly incense wand over him, grinned at him, and bared his reddish-brown, ground-spotted teeth. "You'll be alright, lad. Our stuff works real good." More customers were crowding around. This was live action, especially to the skeptics. So far, it seemed he had swallowed more that 10 ounces of the foul-tasting tea.

"Aghhhhh! Aghhh!" he continued.

"Poor kid, he might need a stronger brew," Ma

Opportuna assumed. She then promptly began to educate her customers, "You see, sometimes you start off with light tea, like I have done for this kid. If it is not getting the job done, you make a much stronger brew. The poor lad might need this. Open your mouth for me, darlin'." TW took another gulp. Taste-bud tragedy! He had never tasted anything so gut-wrenchingly repulsive. His nerves must have just been fried. Goosebumps were all over him, and all of his teeth were suddenly sensitive from the sharp-tasting concoction. He couldn't take one more sip. He had no choice but to call off his self-inflicted terror.

"I'm okay now, Ma Opportuna," he begrudgingly mumbled. Applause instantly erupted, and Pa Opportuna helped the boy off the floor. Orders poured in...twice as many. TW dusted himself off. He felt like an absolute failure. He had promised himself that he would drink that stuff till nightfall, if need be, and never get "cured." But he could no longer bear the impossible taste. To the onlookers, that meant he was healed.

"Sacra tea is really amazing," he heard an impressed customer remark in awe. What in the world had he done! Shame, shame, shame on him! If only the ground could just open and swallow him up. He walked sheepishly out of the kiosk, head bowed down in defeat.

Pa Opportuna had no idea of TW's personal anguish. "He's probably still a little weak," he remarked. "I'll send him home with an amber lantern, and he'll be full of vigor by tomorrow."

"TW, TW!"

Suddenly hearing his name snapped him out of his endless replay of that regretful Saturday event. It was Ma Opportuna calling.

"Me darlin', it's time to pack up and go home. Don't you worry, we'll have great sales again tomorrow. We do have to take a break and get refreshed. I've got an extra cup of freshly brewed sacra tea and some honey wafers. Would you like that?"

"No thanks," TW replied in a resigned voice. He packed up what was left of Aunty Attitudah's petal papyrus, grabbed the handles of the wheelbarrow, and wearily made his way home. Oh yes, he needed to tell his aunt that the hatmaker requested 4 P's.

4

"Desecration! Utter desecration! Totally abhorrent!" cried a disgusted Townsitter as he walked through the marketplace observing Graceville's unbelievable trade. He had come to the marketplace to do his shopping since Cheerlos, the Tempostry-help, was sick. Tea satchets, petals, paper dolls, lanterns, almost anything imaginable was now made from the Sacra Vellum. Townsitters typically didn't come to the marketplace. They spent the majority of their lives in the Tempostry and were not to be seen living a life of finery or frivolity. But perhaps it was a good thing this Townsitter came out to see Graceville's madness. He was reeling from the citizens' brutal audacity. "Where was respect for Imortul? How could they trade like this in the day and sleep in peace at night?" he thought to himself. It was clear that Graceville's precious tradition was quickly becoming extinct. Evidently, the reports they had been receiving at the Tempostry that all was well in Graceville were quite untrue. The marketplace was full of Selfville and Falseburg citizens buying bits and pieces of their most sacred book. A few traders had noticed his astonished expression as he paced up and down the main street. They began to pack up their wares for fear that their goods might be seized. But the Townsitter was too stunned to respond. He needed to get back to the Tempostry; an emergency meeting was critical.

They gathered hastily. With no excuses permitted, all the Townsitters were in attendance. Their grave faces matched their austere surroundings. This included Elder Candy, who never wore anything other than a smiling face. He was the only Townsitter who would venture into the streets on a regular basis; he was Graceville's favorite. He carried a pouch of candy around his neck and would hand out a piece or two to any unhappy face who walked by him saying, "Candeez for a smiley kid?" TW had often come to him for comfort. The friendly Townsitter knew the twelve-year old's unhappy life with Aunt Attitudah and lavished him with more candy than he did any other kid. For the grown-ups, he always had a sweet word of encouragement. In fact, that was why the people named him Elder Candy. Most people didn't even know his real name.

The meeting room was tense. No one had more than a nod or a mutter for his fellow elder. Was there any hope for Graceville's Sacra Vellum? That was the disturbing question on every Elder's mind. All eyes were on the Chief Townsitter. He was a little nervous and kept rubbing the mole on his left eyebrow. He took a deep breath and stood up to address them.

"Fellow Elders," he began, in a most sober tone, "It is obvious to all that we have the most intriguing book in the world, our beloved Sacra Vellum. However, not even the brightest man-made lights have ever been bright enough to reveal its words at the 10 o'clock hour we've been commanded to read. The pages remain blank before us, and we cannot explain why. Despite this fact, we must hope that one day a special light will be sent to us so that we may read its contents and receive our promised joy. It is indeed a mysterious book and has made us a special people. But for now, the people of Graceville are in total despair and tired of being mocked by those from the neighboring towns. If we do not find a way to keep the people of Graceville respectfully holding on to the Sacra Vellum, we will lose our special tradition and ultimately

our sense of worth."

The Townsitters all agreed that since it was impossible to change the laws of darkness, and that attempting to read the book in the day's sunlight would be terrible disobedience to Imortul's 10 o'clock decree, something more attainable would need to be proposed. After hours of debating and reflecting, they came up with what they thought was an incredible idea. It was a plan that they believed would restore Graceville's tradition of honoring their Sacra Vellum. They would pass some new laws to replace those decreed by Imortul. The Townsitters were all excited. Elder Candy's gaping grin returned, and there was laughter, embracing, and enthusiastic chatter around the meeting room. Cheerlos was dispatched to immediately sound the Drum-Comm and alert Graceville of a mandatory assembly.

5

Dum du du du du dum. Dum du du du du dum. The distinct call of drums filled the marketplace. The Townsitters were calling for an immediate gathering. They rarely did. TW suspected it had to do with the Sacra Vellum. The thought of that was enough to excite TW. Hadn't a Townsitter come to the marketplace the day before and expressed horror at the abominable trade? How could it be anything else? In response to the call, he rushed through the marketplace clumsily weaving in and out of traders and customers with his wheelbarrow.

"Oops! I'm sorry." "Pardon me, sir." "Not again!" The wheelbarrow had overturned for the third time. He rushed to scoop the delicate, but now dirty, petals back into the cart. He sighed, disgusted with his clumsiness. "Just what I need to make for a beautiful evening with Aunty Atty!" he sarcastically muttered to himself. He eventually made it home, set the wheelbarrow in Aunty Attitudah's floral shop, and rushed back out into the street. By the time he reached the square, it was evident that this must be a very important meeting. The whole square was abuzz with various discussions, anticipations, restless crying babies, and lots of chatty folk here and there. The Townsitters were fully decorated in their robes and headgear, strutting majestically through the gathering crowd. *Dududum-Dududum.* Absolute silence was called for. In a single moment, the entire crowd hushed to a pin-drop silence. The Chief Townsitter took the stand.

"Dear people of Graceville, you know that we are a very precious people who have a special history unlike anyone else in the world. That history is based on the Sacra Vellum we possess; the book that contains the secrets of joy for us and the whole world. But we also know that a powerful law of nature, which causes darkness at night in our region, has prevented us from reading our beloved book and obeying its words. So, in the end, we are really no different from the people of Falseburg, Selfville, or Angertown. Because of this, some of you have already given up your very precious tradition. But I say to you today, the Townsitters of Graceville, who have been charged with watching over you and our traditions, have come together to make some new laws. These laws will help us truly enjoy the prestige of owning our precious Sacra Vellum and will even keep the Great Imortul closer to our hearts than he ever was."

There were instant shouts of jubilation and sighs of relief among the people. Many of them revered Imortul, though they had never seen him. It would be quite phenomenal to find means of pleasing Imortul, even without reading the book!

"These are the new rules agreed upon by the Townsitters that you must follow," the Chief Townsitter continued. The people instantly hushed. They had waited for this moment all their lives. "First of all, I abolish the sale of any Sacra Vellum ware in our marketplace. Those who participated in such a trade brought darkness to our community, but their ignorance is forgiven."

TW cringed upon hearing this proclamation. He had brought darkness? If only people knew how he really felt. For the next few minutes he faded in and out of all the Chief Townsitter was saying, wallowing in regret and self-pity. Surely he could have stood up to his aunt—even if the price was homelessness. He felt absolutely rotten. He became terribly uncomfortable. Everyone around knew him. They were probably staring at him, too. How it hurt!

A sudden raised pitch in the Chief Townsitter's voice returned his focus to the speech.

"Every night at 10 o'clock, you will gather your family together and sing a song about the special 10 o'clock hour. Then you will place your Sacra Vellum under your pillow as you fall asleep. The pillow must be filled with red-dyed, jasmine-scented, semi-plume feathers to show extra reverence for Imortul. By doing these things, Imortul will see what efforts you have made to stay close to him, even though you cannot read the contents of his book. We will honor him by keeping this ritual at exactly 10 o'clock each night, just as he has commanded. Thank you, and long live the town and the spirit of Graceville." The people of Graceville cheered and gave their Chief Townsitter tokens of appreciation.

6

B*ang, bang, bang, bang*. The cruel banging had become the anticipated interruption to what were once Graceville's quiet nights. Inspectors were at the door. They were hired by the Townsitters to drop in, unannounced, at people's homes at ten at night to ensure that each family was following the new rules precisely. All the people were required to sing the 10 o'clock song to a famous Monkonian tune:

Oh 10 o'clock, Oh 10 o'clock
How lovely is your hour
In years before, and present years
You are the great commander's choice
Oh 10 o'clock, oh 10 o'clock, how lovely is your hour

The Inspectors would often drop in on sleeping families to check underneath their pillows. It wasn't long before the people were once again in despair. Some families began to bribe the Inspectors not to report them when they were forgetful. The Inspectors charged heavy fines for any perceived disobedience. One family had recently suffered a break-in by thieves and had all their pillows stolen. Before they had the chance to buy some new feathered pillows, they were given a "No feathers found" fine. Another family had the flu and could not sing without coughing. Even though this was no fault of theirs, the Inspector was so unforgiving that he fined them for "Singing with insufficient melody." So with sore throats, runny noses, and puffy eyes, they handed him their money. The "Insufficient" category of fines was the most notorious, and brought in the most fortune to the Townsitters. It allowed the Inspectors to fine at their own impulse. Anything could be categorized as "Insufficient." There had been fines such as "Singing with insufficient cheerfulness," "Insufficient pillows per household," "Insufficient jasmine scent wafting out of pillow," and

"Insufficient dedication to the 10 o'clock traditions." It would be surprising to find a family that had not emptied their purses to the Inspectors. The Townsitters, along with the Inspectors, grew more powerful and shamefully corrupt as they decided who would be punished and who would be pardoned.

As time went on, life for Graceville citizens took a turn for the worse. Mothers became further burdened with the extra chore of daily preparing their home for the Inspectors, while fathers became angrier as they felt that their homes were being invaded. Of particular note was the home of Attitudah. She was growing increasingly irritable and sometimes hysterical with the Inspectors. Preferring to pay fines rather than sing the "soppy song," as she called it, she banned them from coming to her doorstep. In addition, there was no way she was going to save the Sacra Vellum under a pillow while it was possible to bring in some income through her, now underground, petal papyrus trade. As she heard the sound of the Inspectors' boots approaching, she would fling her fine out through the window screaming, "Here you go, you lousy nitwits. You'd better not knock on my door!" The coins jingled on the cobblestone outside the window and would roll in different directions. The Inspectors would gather every money-piece in view and shout back that the amount was incomplete. This time she would scream at TW, "Get outside and search for the missing coins and you'd better

find them all!" In what now seemed to be a nightly ritual, TW would be on his hands and knees, straining his eyes in the dark, searching for Aunty Attitudah's lost coins. Typically, TW would find them all, except when it was that dreadful Inspector Jaw on the beat. On those nights, he somehow always came up short by one coin. He would feel a knife-like grip on his shoulder, forcing him up from his knees. Inspector Jaw would then clasp his chin and level it with his cold, scarred face.

"I need that coin now!" his steely voice would threaten TW.

"Yes sir," TW would feebly reply. Then he would quickly thrust his nervous, sweat-filled hand into his waist-pouch and hand the thieving Inspector a coin from his paltry monthly allowance. Because of this, he lost two coins every month for the two times Inspector Jaw was assigned to Aunt Attitudah's street. There was once an unfortunate occasion where he lost a third coin because Inspector Jaw was covering for a co-Inspector who was sick. How much more of this could he possibly bear?

There was no one to whom he could talk. Wasn't he the one who had brought darkness to the community? In school he was a loner. Once, a new boy had joined his class and taken an instant interest in becoming his friend. But by lunchtime, the boy had been updated by the rest of his class. "TW brings darkness. He despises the Sacra Vellum, selling them as paper petals." The boy promptly joined the others and kept his distance.

After school TW remained a loner. He would often roam aimlessly through Graceville's streets and alleys, kicking a pebble here, chasing a rabbit there, looking out for Elder Candy's lollipops, or curiously peering through a window or two searching for entertainment. No one could understand how much he had hated peddling those petals. He really loved the Sacra Vellum, but Aunty Attitudah's greed had sentenced him to a pitiful existence.

While the citizens of Graceville lived in paranoia and despair, the Townsitters and Inspectors grew rich from the fines that were brought in from the forgetful, the sick, and the plundered. The Tempostry entryway was now adorned with an impressive golden arch, crafted by the same builders who built the golden temple of Mee in Selfville. The main doorway no longer revealed a long, dimly lit hallway, but rather a richly decorated foyer complete with several golden animal statues and clusters of delicate lampstands. There was also a rumor that the wooden desks in each of the Townsitters' rooms had been replaced with solid ivory tables. Embroidered pillows, trimmed with plush tassels and stuffed with the custom-ordered feathers from Feathersburg, also decorated each bedroom. Even Feathersburg had begun to prosper due to Graceville's new laws. To honor Imortul, a banquet was held each day which served a variety of delicacies, fine drinks, and famous teas from well beyond the Monkonian

Musing Parlour

region. A highly reputed chef from Powers-on-the-Hill was hired to oversee the preparation of the food and the ornamental arrangement of the banqueting table. Everyone at the Tempostry seemed to be enjoying the lavish lifestyle. Of course, they kept it to themselves since they were required to remain in solitude!

With the exception of the Townsitters and Inspectors, the people of Graceville were in total misery. They seemed even further away from the life of joy that the Sacra Vellum had promised. Many moved out of Graceville to seek a less burdensome life. Others questioned the new laws. Professor Smartee, a historian in one of the local institutions of higher learning, felt that the 10 o'clock at night law wasn't as perplexing as the Townsitters had assumed. "The problem," he said, "was ignorance of Graceville's history." He went on to say that he had evidence that the people of Graceville had migrated northwards from a region near the South Pole where, in the summer, 10 o'clock at night was as bright as 10 o'clock in the day time. Therefore, he proposed reading the Sacra Vellum at 10 o'clock in the morning to compensate for the emigration disadvantage. Every afternoon he gave a *Lecture of Understanding* right outside Graceville's Musing Parlor.

Additionally, there were many other arguments, ideas, and occasional protests, and even rebel attacks. Some of the youth formed a group known as the Graceville Pollinators. They would often wait in dark alleys to spray the Inspectors with pollen spray as they headed to their 10 o'clock inspections. The Inspectors would instantly have massive allergy attacks. Sneezing and coughing, with red and teary eyes, they would have to give up on inspections for the night. Graceville was truly falling apart!

7

"Cheap tickets! Cheap tickets! Get the 'Sitters' noose off your neck! Join the mass exodus out of Graceville." Freedom-bound Transport Services had this advertisement slammed across the center pages of the *Graceville Times*. It was a direct challenge to the Townsitters and their new laws.

Pa and Ma Opportuna were some of the first to respond. TW had been walking home from school when he heard, "TW! It's Ma Opportuna." She was calling from a Freedom-bound wagon. "Oh, ma boy, see how miserable you look! It's a terrible thing they aren't allowing us to sell our Sacra Vellum wares. I can see the sadness all over your face, me darlin'. Can you imagine they called us 'darkness?' Pa and me are heading to Selfville to see if we can start a new business there. If not, then Angertown, but definitely not here. This place has become so terrible. We were all doing so well with our Sacra Vellum wares. Anyway, if you need us, just look for us. We'll be in the marketplace over there," she pointed in the direction of the west mountains and continued to talk on and on. But TW was not listening anymore and just kept on walking.

Everyday brought fresh lines of people to the wagon stand, each one waiting for a seat on the Freedom-bound.

"There goes another wagon filled with our citizens," muttered Elder Debtson as he peered through the Tempostry banqueting room window and observed a squeaky-wheeled wagon heading off into the distance. He looked at the Chief Townsitter, awaiting a response to his observation. But the Townsitter remained quiet. It could be that he was muted by the heavy load of food he had just consumed for dinner.

"I saw quite a number of your citizens at the Festival of Mee," added the Powers-on-the-Hill Chef to both Townsitters as he served them freshly brewed tea. "I would say at least seventy."

"Seventy!" shouted the Chief Townsitter, visibly

alarmed by the Chef's statement.

"We did hear that Freedom-bound Transport Services ran an advertisement encouraging citizens to 'join the mass exodus out of Graceville,'" Elder Debtson reminded the Chief.

"Yes, but you know anything in the *Times* is sensational. Who'd want to believe it?" replied the Chief. "What are we going to do? This is a very serious matter. It's bad enough that they are leaving Graceville, but even worse, they are showing up at the Festival of Mee. Imortul will certainly not be pleased with the way we are preserving our people and their love for the Sacra Vellum. We must meet immediately."

"I do hear loud snores, Chief," the Chef quickly interjected. "It appears some have retired to bed early. Can I have a banquet ready for you mid-morning tomorrow?"

"Yes, that would be perfectly fine. Inform Cheerlos, when he comes in to clean up, that he is to make all the Elders aware of this urgent meeting." At that, he left the banqueting room with Elder Debtson following closely behind.

"Elder Debtson," the Chef called just before he exited the doorway. "I've brought you eight secret power books. Any idea when you will be paying for them?" Elder Debtson's protruding stomach filled the doorway. He released a loud voluminous burp and chewed hard on the toothpick hanging from the side of his mouth, thinking for a moment.

"Um, I have it in mind to pay you. Just give me a few more days. But don't let that stop you from bringing the next two in the series. By the way, bring some happi-drink to my room when you are done."

"Yes sir. I brought you one of Powers-on-the-Hill's finest. I will also add its price to the total amount you owe on the books."

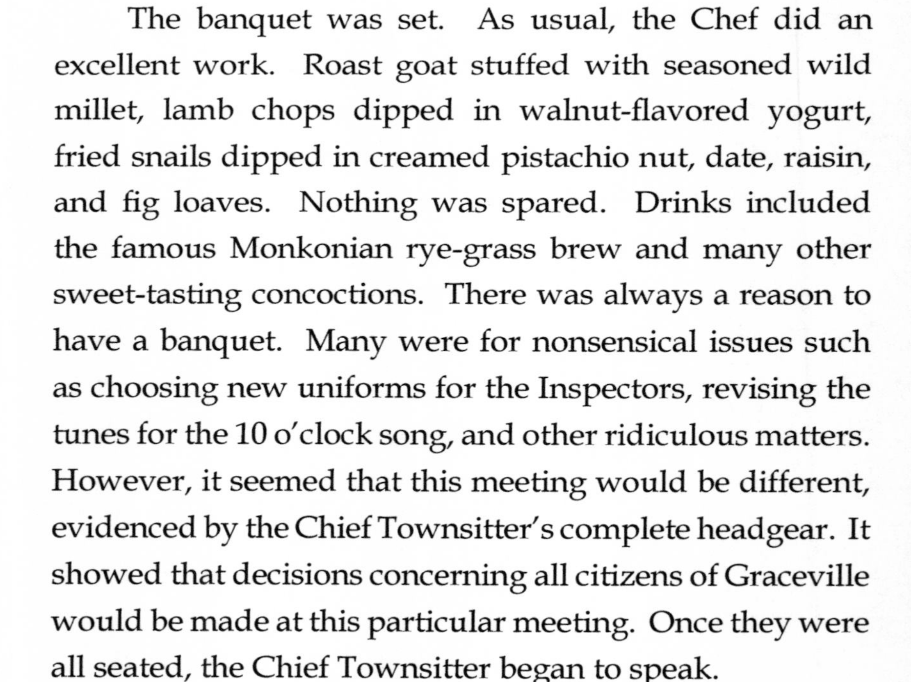
The banquet was set. As usual, the Chef did an excellent work. Roast goat stuffed with seasoned wild millet, lamb chops dipped in walnut-flavored yogurt, fried snails dipped in creamed pistachio nut, date, raisin, and fig loaves. Nothing was spared. Drinks included the famous Monkonian rye-grass brew and many other sweet-tasting concoctions. There was always a reason to have a banquet. Many were for nonsensical issues such as choosing new uniforms for the Inspectors, revising the tunes for the 10 o'clock song, and other ridiculous matters. However, it seemed that this meeting would be different, evidenced by the Chief Townsitter's complete headgear. It showed that decisions concerning all citizens of Graceville would be made at this particular meeting. Once they were all seated, the Chief Townsitter began to speak.

"Fellow Elders," he looked around the room acknowledging each of them with a sober nod, "it has come to my attention that many are leaving Graceville." He was interrupted by snorts, burps, and disinterested sighs. But he ignored them and continued, "It is evident that since we created the new laws for our people to make the Sacra Vellum their most hallowed possession, Imortul has shown his pleasure by lavishing us with much wealth and comfort. Just look around you." The Chief Townsitter motioned all to look around themselves. Indeed, it was plain to see the opulence around the banquet table—ironically tasteless too—they were adorned with thick velvet robes decked with mismatched tassels, trims, and odd-shaped bits and pieces. Around their necks looked like a treasure chest of tangled jewelry. They admired one another and beamed, obviously impressed at Imortul's seeming reward. Gaining their attention, the Chief continued, "Some of our citizens prefer lawlessness, choosing to leave Graceville and join in the temple worship of Mee; creating new opportunities to serve their appetites rather than faithfully pleasing Imortul. We need to stop this exodus immediately. If they leave, what will happen to us? What you enjoy now will soon be no more. So we must wisely revise the laws to keep them here."

Elder Candy was aghast at what he had just heard. He flung his napkin over his uneaten meal and pushed himself away from the table. They were willing to revise the laws, not because they feared losing Graceville's Sacra Vellum, but to protect their power over the people and their growing wealth. In his heart he had never felt right about these banquets, and he had only endured them out of duty. He was not going to tolerate them any further. "This is unjust!" he cried in total disgust. "Graceville has become a miserable town because of these new and burdensome laws. If Imortul has said that his Sacra Vellum must only be read at 10 o'clock while knowing that it is impossible for us to do so, perhaps it is time to ask him what kind of light will reveal its pages, rather than make up laws for the people. None of us here sing the 10 o'clock song, so why should the people?" He had barely finished his statement when another full-mouthed Townsitter angrily interrupted.

"You are speaking nonsense! The generations before us have tried every type of light there is, and nothing has worked. Even the most powerful lamps have not revealed one word on the pages of that book. Let us proceed with revising the law according to our pleasure."

"I will not be a part of this injustice!" Elder Candy furiously stormed out of the meeting. As he made his exit, the door-frame hook cruelly caught the candy pouch around his neck, spilling lollipops across the doorway.

8

Elder Candy didn't have the heart to walk through the town. None of the kids, not even TW, took his candy anymore. When he offered his lollipops, they simply shunned him and walked off. No sweet word he said could bring a smile to anyone's face. In his heart, he knew that the wealth from the fines was nothing compared to the happiness he had received from watching little kids walk away from him with lollipops in their hands, and great big grins across their faces. With nowhere else to go, he wandered down the back streets until he came to Lonely

Hill. It was just as its name described: lonely. There was a strange story about this hill. On the top were three wooden stumps. No one was quite sure how they got there. They were as mysterious as Graceville's Sacra Vellum. Because of that mystery, no one really came around there, so it was the perfect getaway spot for Elder Candy.

Weary and miserable, he tore his rich robe and cried, "Great Imortul, if you are there and the people of Graceville are precious to you, then come down and rescue us and give us the life and joy you promised us." He fell on his face with aching sobs and wept bitterly for all that was happening in his beloved town. He wept until, in complete exhaustion, he fell asleep.

A soft touch upon his shoulders woke him. He rose up, startled. He wasn't sure how long he had been there, but he was so hungry. A stranger with a kind smile and a food basket was standing above him. "Who are you?" the Elder inquired. Before the stranger could reply, a famished Elder Candy moaned, "I'm starving. I need to get to the marketplace before nightfall." He struggled weakly to his feet, adjusting his robe.

"I do have some fig loaves, fruit, and a flask of sweet drink. I'll be happy to share with you," the stranger quickly responded as he opened his basket. Elder Candy looked at the beautifully packed food and smiled at the stranger in gratitude. In seconds, he was wolfing down the delicious food. The stranger continued, "As I was

touring our world, I was stopped by two Tear Fellows. One named Oppressed, the other named Desperate. They said you had wept them out from you and were on their way to present your futile condition before Imortul.

Elder Candy frowned. "I certainly didn't talk to anyone out here. No one comes to Lonely Hill. In fact, I'm surprised you're here. So who were these people I supposedly sent?" By this time, Elder Candy had stopped eating. He had become guarded, not knowing what this absurd conversation was all about.

"The Tear Fellows are servants of Imortul. They reside in all his people, and gain their voice when they are wept out. Once they are out, they have one mission. They must seek the only advocate who can plead their cause before the great Imortul," the stranger informed him.

"So what has that got to do with you?" Elder Candy questioned suspiciously, "Judging from your humble appearance, you certainly cannot be the majestic great commander."

"My name is Messenger Joygive. I am from Imortul, and I have come to help you." He pulled out a gold-covered Sacra Vellum from beneath his faded cloak. The Elder's eyes shot wide open with excitement and hope.

"Do you want to hear my story?" he hastily interjected. The two sat together as the troubled Elder poured out the recent events of Graceville to Messenger Joygive.

"I would like to read the Sacra Vellum to all of

Graceville. Can you arrange an assembly?"

"What do you mean?" Elder Candy asked, puzzled. "There is no light that shines brightly enough to read the pages in that book. We've tried all that we can, and even after obtaining the most powerful lights from the world's best light-makers, its words still cannot be seen." He paused for a moment to think about the stranger's proposition. This was all very strange. He was just told he had resident tears which were apparently flushed out when he wept. Somehow, those tears had "spoken" about his misery with this very strange man. Most impressive of all, the stranger actually owned a Sacra Vellum! No one else outside Graceville was known to possess a sacra Vellum, let alone a gold one! Could he really take the risk and believe this stranger? What was the worst that could happen? He was already in a bad situation. He sighed, "I will arrange for the assembly. After all, we are hopeless." With that, both of them arose and headed down the hill toward Graceville.

9

Du du du du dum dum. The Drum Comm was calling for a meeting again. TW looked up from his composition notebook. He had been doodling on the page, struggling with whether he could actually answer what the composition topic asked: "What is the biggest struggle of your heart?" Could he dare write the truth? The Drum Comm was a welcoming distraction.

He could see his aunt in a quiet corner of her workroom, secretly crafting petals for a waiting merchant from Selfville. Attitudah's petals were very popular with the Selfites, so when the new law abolished Sacra Vellum trading, Selfville merchants asked if she could continue to make them secretly. This, she was happy to continue. She got a steady supply of free Sacra Vellums from the wagon stand. "You won't need these where you are going. I'll be happy to relieve you of the extra load," she would say to the despondent emigrants as they got in line to board the wagon. She paid enough fines to keep the Inspectors out of her house, and twice a week the merchant would arrive to pick up the wares. They would then leave Graceville with boxes of petal papyrus under the cover of darkness.

"What do they want this time?" she huffed in irritation at the interrupting Drum Comm.

"Aunty Attitudah, it's calling for a nine o'clock gathering at the Town Square."

"Let me take what you've got so far. I must leave before the crowd starts to gather," the Selfite merchant said nervously. Attitudah had barely packaged his purchase for him before he grabbed them and dashed out into the night.

People hurriedly completed their duties in response to the sudden call to assemble. What in the world was going on in Graceville this time? If nothing else, they would, for one night, be spared the pounding on their doors by Inspectors. Any means to avoid singing and pillow inspections would be a huge welcome.

Every kind of emotion filled the air in the square

that night: anger, hopelessness, confusion, nervousness, scoffing and, most of all, misery. TW observed the procession of Townsitters as they majestically made their way into the center of the square. Judging from their full regalia, he was sure this had to be a very important meeting. "What were they whispering about?" TW wondered.

Suddenly, one of them laughed out loud in a mocking tone, "This so-called stranger must be a trickster from Falseburg. You know those people can put up an impressive act without thinking. Well, I guess we need to honor the old 'Sitter and let him call for this assembly, ridiculous as it sounds. As if shaming himself in the Tempostry wasn't sufficient, he's calling for double shame. He'll get it. His heart deceives him into thinking that anyone can read the Sacra Vellum. He's going insane just because the kids aren't taking his candy anymore." TW could not believe his ears. He wasn't really sure what the Townsitters were saying, but he was shocked at their irreverent tone. He'd have to wait to see what would be revealed at this assembly.

There were five minutes left till 10 o'clock, when Elder Candy took the stand. "People of Graceville, I will now introduce to you a kind stranger, whom I met today while in a sorrowful state on that deserted hill just beyond Graceville. I was surprised at his knowledge of Imortul and his deep understanding of Graceville's history, since some are secrets, known only within the walls of the Tempostry. I was persuaded that such a being would be trustworthy enough to bring into your presence. The purpose for which I have brought him is to perform the phenomenal feat of reading the Sacra Vellum, which he assured me he would do in your presence at 10 o'clock tonight. If he can accomplish this act, which is so unimaginable to us, Graceville will undoubtedly enter into a new era. We would be considered the most privileged of all Graceville's generations to witness this ageless hope. Let us warmly receive this kind stranger in the spirit of Graceville's hospitality." At that, he ushered the kind stranger to the stand.

When the people saw that he was a humble man, dressed in a fairly-worn tunic, certainly far from the royalty that would be expected of any messenger from Imortul, if there was such a thing, some snickered. Others coughed mischievously, some rolled their eyeballs, and the Townsitters tilted their noses upward with haughty expressions. As soon as the Town Square clock chimed 10 o'clock, the man spoke. His authoritative tone got the attention of all.

"Imortul has sent me to tell you to cease from your striving. The Sacra Vellum cannot be read by the earth's light, whether by day or by night. You may turn off all your lamps and every light source which you have brought with you tonight. None will be needed." Out of curiosity, and also due to fear of the Elders, everyone turned off their lights. With a moonless sky above their heads, the whole square was thrown into total darkness. Except for pounding hearts, the entire assembly was absolutely still. Breaking the silence, the man spoke the first words ever heard from the Sacra Vellum:

"The care and the concern that you show towards yourself, show such care and concern to all others."

Nothing like this had been heard before in all of Graceville's history. He spoke many amazing words out of their beloved book which brought a special warmth and peace over the people. Peace that their troubled hearts had never before experienced. When he had finished, he asked them to turn on their lights and lamps.

Awe and wonder filled the assembly. "How could he have read it without the light? How could he have read in the midst of the darkness?" they wondered in amazement amongst themselves. Many of the Townsitters, though, were incensed and spoke loudly against him.

"He's a hoax, a fraud; he's here from Falseburg in search of cheap fame," the Elders shouted. They feared that this strange man had come to destroy the system that had made them rich and powerful, and immediately began to order the people back to their homes. They yelled angrily at the peaceful stranger, "We are the custodians of the Sacra Vellum, and we will decide how we want the people of Graceville to understand it!" In their fury, they began to violently usher him away from the Town Square bellowing, "Leave our town! Get out of our town! You are not welcome here!" A couple of Townsitters beckoned the Inspectors to take over and finish the cruel job of removing him from the town. At least a dozen Inspectors swarmed the stranger, immediately isolating him from the inquiring crowd of confused people who were hoping to learn more. Some Inspectors pushed the crowd away, threatening unpardonable fines and various punishments if they did not immediately leave. Other Inspectors viciously dragged the stranger away, shouting many unkind words at him. However, the stranger did not answer them. He said nothing until he found a momentary pause between their venomous curses. He turned towards the harassed crowd.

"I am Messenger Joygive, sent from Imortul, your great commander. If anyone wants to read and enjoy the treasures of the Sacra Vellum, meet me tomorrow night at Lonely Hill. The lights of this world will never show the words of Imortul, but brightness will proceed from Imortul himself, lighting up the pages and revealing the words of your treasured Sacra Vellum to every willing heart. You will read just as I read, and no one will ever be able take that light away from you." Suddenly, a thick ball of mucousy spit which was forcefully ejected from Inspector Jaw's mouth, landed squarely on Messenger Joygive's forehead.

"Dull-brained swindler. Get out!"

TW recoiled at the beastly action. "Hypocrite," he muttered, his fist clenched in anger, wishing he could strike out at Inspector Jaw. But, he was certain, that would be his death sentence. In wide-eyed terror, he anticipated what would happen next. He looked in the direction where the Townsitters had gathered. They stood aloof, observing from a distance the reckless treatment being inflicted on the Graceville visitor. Their looks clearly communicated that they approved of the assault. In their opinion, anyone who claimed to be able to read the Sacra Vellum should also have the power to protect himself. Otherwise, he was nothing but a fraud. "Where was Elder Candy?" TW thought as his eyes roamed the square, giving up hope that assistance would come from any of the other Townsitters.

"Stop this insanity! Stop it!" yelled an angry Elder Candy. He had been desperately trying to break through the chain of brutal Inspectors. They dispersed upon hearing his fierce command, allowing him access to the stranger. Elder Candy promptly pulled out a handkerchief from his candy pouch to wipe off the filthy contents from his guest's forehead. "I am so sorry to have put you through all this, sir," he apologized, thoroughly embarrassed and ashamed of Graceville's barbaric behavior. He turned angrily to the Inspectors, "You are dismissed!"

Elder Candy continued to apologize profusely as he led Messenger Joygive away from the square. The following crowd had died down in response to the Inspectors' threats, but TW crept slowly behind, within ear shot. Elder Candy caught sight of him. "It is for miserable folk like this that my heavy heart was compelled to invite you here tonight. They need hope. We all need help. There is more to Graceville than brutal Inspectors and suspicious Townsitters. Please keep your word to us and visit us at Lonely Hill tomorrow, just as you said earlier."

"Oh, I most certainly will. Graceville has no heart hardened enough to restrain me. It will be my pleasure to receive your people at Lonely Hill." Elder Candy was clearly stunned by Messenger Joygive's compassionate response. How could he not be vengeful after such great insults?

"Thank you, sir," he stuttered; quite embarrassed that he was requesting favors after witnessing the despicable treatment of his guest. "Can I provide you with a bed for the night?"

"No, you need not worry. I have rest that I obtain through the service of Imortul. I am continually refreshed as I serve him. A bed will not be necessary tonight. I will see you at Lonely Hill tomorrow." At that, Messenger Joygive bade Elder Candy a firm goodnight and walked into the moonless night toward the hill. TW had heard the entire conversation. He had to get to that hill! His heart was pounding as he raced homeward.

As he made his way through the back streets, he heard various reactions to the amazing event that had just occurred. One thing was clear — the Graceville community was split about whether to trust this stranger. Some who were fearful concluded they would continue the book-under-pillow tradition. "It was safer that way," they reasoned. They would be law abiding citizens and receive the approval of the Townsitters. Others decided they had been miserable long enough; they believed it was worth the risk to follow the kind stranger. Perhaps they would even get to read the Sacra Vellum! Small groups of people were scattered around the square and on the streets, either convincing others or waiting to be convinced by others, about the genuineness of Messenger Joygive.

10

It was almost thirty minutes past the hour of eleven by the time TW got home. Judging from the lamps lit in the main window, his aunt was home. He wasn't sure if she had gone to the square or not, but that was another matter. TW bravely went up to her. He really wanted to be at Lonely Hill. This stranger's message seemed to be the best news he had ever heard. He not only wanted to ask her permission to go, but he really wanted her to be there, too. After all, in spite of everything, she was still his aunt and cared enough to give him a roof over his head. Even more importantly, she might be convinced that the Sacra Vellum could be read rather than be used for profit. His heart was pounding, and he could feel a large lump rising in his throat. He knew he only had one chance to persuade her. "Aunty Attitudah," he began in a nervous near-whisper. "Remember how you always say that my father, your brother, hoped to live to see the day when the Sacra Vellum would be read in all of Graceville? Do you think he would be honored if we make the effort to fulfill his hope?" He had finished in a confident and more convincing tone. Attitudah had been bent over at the table, heavily concentrating on making some polka-dotted petunias petal papyrus, a favorite of the Selfites. When she heard his words, she straightened up. There was a not-so-callous emotion across her face which was quite a rarity.

She looked intently at TW, "If you feel that this act will honor your father, you have my permission to go. As for me, I don't know what I will do." TW was elated. He couldn't believe his ears. His aunt, who had despised the Sacra Vellum, was actually going to allow him visit Lonely Hill. This was incredible!

"Thanks Aunty Attitudah," he quickly said, wanting to scurry off, as if lingering a moment longer would cause her to reconsider. But as he backed off, he tripped and landed on a chest in the corner of the room that was stacked with several Sacra Vellums, awaiting the guillotine. "I'm sorry, Aunty," he muttered sheepishly. He straightened up and immediately bent over to retrieve the several books scattered across the floor. His initials! His Sacra Vellum! How did it get here? His heart was beating like it would burst through his chest. The accidental chilling discovery of his very own Sacra Vellum awaiting his aunt's guillotine had rattled him to the core. "Oh no!" an emotional whisper of disbelief escaped his lips. His dreaded fear of losing his sacred book was about to become a reality. This would be the end of his precious Sacra Vellum. He grabbed his book from the floor and hugged it tightly against his chest. "Aunty, this is mine! It's mine!" choked TW, clearly anguished. He was staring at her intently, angry, and at the same time fearful. He had his doubts that she would show any pity.

"I see," she mumbled, not stopping to raise her head. "That must have been the one that fell out of the roof today when I went up to rescue the neighbor's cat. I consider it a lucky find. I need it anyway; otherwise, I'll be short for my next delivery to the Selfites."

"No, Aunty! No!" TW wailed desperately. Tears were streaming down his face now. As expected, his pain didn't gain any sympathy from his aunt. Her face was intently set on the work before her, totally ignoring his plight. As far as she was concerned, the Sacra Vellum was truly good for nothing but profit. He stood there for what seemed minutes on end, hoping she'd change her mind.

But she just kept working. "Please, Aunty, pleeease!" he attempted a more desperate plea.

"You're never going to be able to read it. Hand it over to me and be off to bed now, boy," she responded coldly. He was trembling fiercely. He couldn't believe this was happening to him—the very day before he believed he would read his own Sacra Vellum. He had to persuade her with something more impressive than his fruitless wails. All of a sudden he wiped his tears away, then standing up tall in quite a drastic change in disposition, he mustered up a bright and cheery tone.

"Hey, Aunty, pretend you've turned my Sacra Vellum into petals. But I'll spare you the labor in doing so; just let me go ahead and pay you for them. I'll be your first pre-cut petals customer." She flung her head backwards and responded with a sarcastic laugh.

"You couldn't pay me if you tried. Your attempt is admirable though." TW was encouraged that she was at least responding. He had no minute to waste on self-pity. He'd have to bargain smartly to fight for his Sacra Vellum.

"Okay, Aunty, you're right. Perhaps I couldn't pay for all the petals. How about giving me a family discount in the name of your brother?" He held his breath. Did he convince her? And if he did, could he really pay?

"With all the petal papyrus you've sold for me, it's a wonder that you're still this passionate about the Sacra

Vellum. I guess I'll consider your bargain. But it's going to cost you. I can't imagine you'll have anything left in your money pouch. Go ahead and pay me for a dozen's worth of petal papyrus." TW quickly unlatched his money pouch from his waist belt, emptied the coins into the cup of his hand—it looked like Inspector Jaw had sealed his doom! Nevertheless, he nervously began to count—it was clearly a pointless effort. Attitudah impatiently interrupted his hopeless exercise. "You'll never have enough!" she screeched. "Take your Sacra Vellum. It's amazing you'd make yourself so poor just to own this meaningless book. Now be gone."

"Thanks, Aunty! And no, I wouldn't have made myself poorer in the way you think of it. I've had to learn how to let go." Inspector Jaw had provided that training! He grabbed his Sacra Vellum and hugged it tightly against his chest. He closed his eyes to savor the moment. "I actually feel much richer." He went out of the room, shuddering at the thought of what almost befell him.

11

The next day, the town was abuzz with debate, anxiety, angry Townsitters, and hopeful citizens. "Hello there! Are you going to the hill today?" was the common greeting of the day. The Elders held an emergency meeting at the Tempostry with only Elder Candy defecting. The Inspectors were also there to get their next orders. The whole town was alive with anticipation of something that had never happened in the history of Graceville. Would Graceville's citizens really read the Sacra Vellum for themselves without the use of any light? The mysterious stranger had invited all willing citizens to the foot of Lonely Hill that evening. Some said they had heard him say that all who came to the hill would be served a special dinner of baked buttermilk rolls, raisin cakes, an assortment of grilled fish, and a variety of grape juices. The people had never received anything for free in their lifetime. Hadn't they often paid much more for things than they were actually worth? And now this! It was also rumored that they would be served by Freshelons, Imortul's royal waiters sent to refresh mortal-beings. It sounded too good to be true. "Free food served by cosmic waiters?" the people wondered cautiously. Perhaps this would turn out to be one cruel joke. However, when they looked in the faces of the wicked Inspectors, they knew it'd be worth the risk. As day turned to dusk, families began to make their journey to the outskirts of the city where Lonely Hill stood. Some had packed along their strongest lights.

"Just in case that dear man needs us to assist with lighting tonight," Grandma Selfayde rationalized.

Those who were headed to the hill were horrified to see that a group of Inspectors had gated the hill. They had set up an inspection table at the only road leading to Lonely Hill. Everyone was rashly questioned and told that their name must be registered. There would be a record of every person leaving Graceville. The Hopelett family arrived at the gate, and it was their turn to be questioned:

"Where are you headed to?" snarled a mean-looking

ALL HALT!

Inspector.

"To Lonely Hill where I will read my Sacra Vellum with my family," stuttered Mr. Hopelett on behalf of his family.

"Do you realize that you could be banished from Graceville if you turn your backs on the laws of the Townsitters?" the Inspector threatened.

"That's quite acceptable," replied Mr. Hopelett, in a more confident tone. "Staying out of Graceville is a small price to pay. While I lived under the law of the Elders in our town, I was miserable. You ruined my family financially by charging us heavy fines when, due to no fault of our own, we could not sing. You've taken everything from us, and there's nothing more to lose." He then ushered his family through the gate towards the hill.

Every family going through the gate had a similar story of misery to tell. Most of them, like TW, had nothing more to lose and did not fear the threats of the Inspectors. Some did, though. One of them was Elder Debtson. As he reached the gates, the Inspectors bowed respectfully. Then one of them spoke up.

"Sir," he said, "If you go through this gate, you will lose your prestigious title as a Townsitter in Graceville. You will no longer be able to call assemblies, speak to the people, or command them as you please. Your name will be removed from the Tempostry and you will be treated as a banished Graceville citizen." Elder Debtson thought for awhile. This was a tense moment for him. Could he really afford to lose the abundant benefits he enjoyed as an Elder? Yet, even with all these, he was quite miserable still. He felt he had found hope in this new fellow who had miraculously read the Sacra Vellum at the assembly. In the end, his status and the resulting pleasures were of greater importance to him; with deep regret, he turned back into Graceville.

The night sky had settled over Lonely Hill. The families sat in circles munching second and third helpings of the delicious dinner served by the Freshelons. They were strange beings, indeed. Pairs of little glowing hands would stealthily appear out of nowhere, set a dish before them, and instantly vanish. Everyone was amazed. The children would run to grasp them, only to catch the air between their fingers. They quickly made a game of chasing after the Freshelons, or as one little girl called them, "fire fingers." "...because they're like fire flies," she cleverly reasoned. The name caught on quickly, and soon there were squeals of laughter erupting from every corner of the hill as little children played with the "fire fingers." This was truly a dream feast. Messenger Joygive had been going around to each family circle, comforting them in all their troubles. How happy these citizens were. There was excitement all around.

Although he sat and ate alone, TW could not have

wished for a better experience. He tucked his Sacra Vellum close to his heart. He found himself saddened that his aunt had not come.

"Hello, TW!" The voice startled him. Who cared to call his name? He quickly swung his head toward the crouching person. Messenger Joygive!

"How in the world did he know my name?" he wondered. The next word he heard shocked him even more.

"I like the curl in the middle of your forehead. It makes you quite special," Messenger Joygive complimented, wearing a broad smile.

"No," stuttered TW, in total disbelief, "that curl is the very thing everyone hates about me. It makes me stick out as the bad kid who brought darkness into Graceville by despising the Sacra Vellum." It was a painful confession. He lowered his head in shame.

Giving him an affectionate hug, Messenger Joygive replied, "Well, I need to let you know that it is those who are of a hardened heart that bring darkness. As for your curl, it can begin to identify you as a Sacra Vellum champion."

"Really?" questioned TW in wide-eyed excitement.

"Yes, really," chuckled Messenger Joygive as he rose to his feet. A cosmic waiter reappeared to serve TW some dessert.

Supernatural things were happening so naturally!

There was much joy in the air, but nothing could compare to the greatest anticipation of all: the reading of their precious book. Every now and then the people glanced at their time pieces as they waited for the town clock in the distance to chime 10 o'clock. Messenger Joygive had promised that all who came would be given a special light in their heart, enabling them to see Imortul's words.

12

Finally the hour arrived. Messenger Joygive rose up in their midst. "It's 10 o'clock!" he cried out loud. "Open your book, and even in the midst of this night's darkness you will see the precious words you've waited for all your lives." With hearts racing, each grabbed their Sacra Vellum. And behold, they read! It was awesomely staggering! The words were written with deep-red ink in very unusual un-Monkonian calligraphy. How was this happening? Grandma Selfayde choked back a tear of adoration as she dropped several lights to the ground. Her help was not needed to make it happen. She was totally dependent on the kindness of this special man for whom she had done nothing. How she earned this privilege, she could only wonder. This was truly miraculous!

"Exponentially fascinating!" were the high sounding words from Professor Smartee. He had originally come to the hill just to record the historic event, but now he was truly humbled. Even he could not explain how, with absolute darkness all around, they could see the words of Imortul so clearly. Suddenly, all his emigration theories were as good as dust. Gasps of amazement filled the night sky as people turned the pages of the Sacra Vellum and read for themselves what no one from Graceville had ever seen before now. Wide-eyed expressions of awe were on every face around the hill.

With a cry of pure joy, and with arms outstretched in wonder, the previously troubled Elder Candy asked, "Why do we see?"

Messenger Joygive replied, "Imortul has seen how you desire his special words above all man-made laws and conveniences. He has given his light to every willing heart so you can read these precious words." Then he explained further, "This is the only way to read the secrets of Imortul. It cannot be bought, nor can it be earned. He gives the light to those who truly desire to receive it. Imortul had given the decree that you could only read the book at 10 o'clock knowing that you would try hard, give

up, and call for help. Yet, for so long, nobody called for help. Instead, many abandoned the Sacra Vellum or made new laws for themselves. Just a few days ago, the great commander heard the bitter cry for help from one of your Townsitters, Elder Candy, and he directed my path to give you the true light for the Sacra Vellum. From now on, read the loving words of Imortul, obey him, and you will know the secrets of life and joy. When you go back into Graceville, share your light with anyone who comes your way."

The families rejoiced, and even the Graceville Pollinators let off some celebratory firecrackers. There would be no need for pollen spray attacks anymore. There was singing throughout the night, and many spent the late hours eagerly reading their newfound treasure.

Eventually, one concerned citizen stood up and said, "We can't live on this hill forever, and we have been banished from our homes in Graceville. We need more help."

Messenger Joygive replied, "You are helped. Return to Graceville at your pleasure. Imortul will send an unseen companion to be with you. You have already read of him in your Sacra Vellum. He is the Optima Dona." Then he spoke his final words, "I will go over the hill to the place of Imortul and tell him that his dream for Graceville has finally come true." Then, in the blink of an eye, he was gone.

13

A loud shriek filled the sky. It came from none other than... Attitudah! She threw off her hat, pulled the pins out of her hair, and screamed, "I'm done for! I'm done for! This is a very terrible thing happening to me. Why, oh why, did I come out here?" she moaned loudly and pitifully. "It is that scallywag of a nephew who caused all this. Where is he, where is that nincompoop of a boy?"

"She's here!" TW gasped with mixed emotions as he heard her shout. There was no one more distinctly hysterical than his aunt. His heart sank. What he ought to be rejoicing over left him terrified. Was he to go to her, or not? It was too dark for her to spot his curl, so he quickly scampered toward Elder Candy for protection. Surely Elder Candy would care for him—he hoped.

Attitudah had not only caused such a fearful reaction in TW, but she seemed to have infected almost everyone on the hill. A few sobs here, some whines there, regretful hisses and deep sighs everywhere. The excitement and confidence brought by the 10 o'clock reading was fading fast, giving way to anxious thoughts of the unknown future. Elder Candy was once again overwhelmed. How would he calm an eccentric like Attitudah? How would he encourage all these people who had suddenly given way to fear?

He heard TW's fierce whisper from right behind him, "Messenger Joygive said he would help us, didn't he?" As the Elder pondered the question, he looked toward the three stumps as if hoping Messenger Joygive would be there again. Then, he saw something. A glowing something! What was that? The center stump suddenly appeared to be glowing. Tuning out all the whining, fearful noises, he curiously and expectantly made his way toward it. Others who saw his curious stare started looking in the same direction. It seemed to be real, because he heard other acknowledgements of the strange activity.

"What's that? Look at that strange glow!" a group called out.

"At least this would be a great way to quiet everyone," the Elder thought. "People of Graceville, look over there!" he shouted as he pointed in the direction of the stumps. Suddenly the hillside was quiet. Even if the silence lasted only for a moment, Elder Candy was grateful for it. Perhaps he'd have a minute to plan the next move. Then an even stranger thing began to happen. The glow took on new form. It was like a circular light rainbow on the stump. People gasped and clutched one another upon witnessing yet another strange occurrence.

"Bizarre, indeed bizarre," commented the historian in quite a puzzled tone.

The next thing that happened could only be described as phenomenal. *Whoosh!* Thousands of Freshelons suddenly erupted from around the glowing stump, flitting and dancing into the crowd of people like butterflies let loose from a crowded cage.

"Are they coming to calm us with more food?" asked one astonished fellow. The Freshelons were moving through and above the crowd. They were soundless and weightless. Their form was obscured by a thick, glowing halo that surrounded each of them. They were not disappearing, and they brought no food this time. What happened next was by far the biggest surprise of all. A Freshelon landed weightlessly upon the shoulder of screaming Attitudah. Her hysteria stopped almost immediately. In an instance, the Freshelon was gone.

Suddenly, Attitudah gave a cry of delight.

"Oh, I smell the loveliest roses. I smell the morning glory, and, ah, what a beautiful scent of periwinkles, daisies, and buttercups. This is delightful! My heart has never known such joy. What a beautiful evening!" She gathered the hem of her skirt into her hand and began to laugh and dance in circles, singing a little made-up tune, "Tra la la la la la, my joy has come, my joy is here!"

Then came another voice, "Oh, I hear the sound of the most exquisite symphony!" This time the cry came from Mr. Lorner, the elementary school music teacher. A Freshelon had just danced off his collar. It seemed that the normal nocturnal noises of the hillside had been transformed into a symphony orchestra just for him. "This is such a joyful moment. I wouldn't trade this experience for anything," he sighed.

The glowing beings jumped from one shoulder to another and another. Each citizen came away with a joyful experience. Even the children were not left out. They felt as though they had been transported to a candy factory!

"I smell banana-flavored lollipops," cried one in excitement.

"Butterscotch flavor, my favorite," squealed another.

"Watermelon and blueberries," added TW. It seemed that his friends were beginning to welcome him, too. The laughing children formed a little circle chanting a silly

rhyme:

All the lollipop flavors are ours –
apples, bananas,
no table-side manners!

"This is great!" shouted Elder Candy. "How marvelous, how glorious!" he laughed out loud. Energy had filled his steps, and he marched up and down the hill rejoicing over the many mysterious outbreaks of joy. This had to be the Help that Messenger Joygive had spoken about.

TW ran toward him and screeched, "Look at my Aunty! She's so happy. No one has ever seen her so happy." Elder Candy stood still and observed her for a minute, beaming. Could this really be Attitudah? No one ever dressed as flamboyantly as she did. Besides, all those paper petals adorning her dress easily gave her away. She spotted TW and Elder Candy and waved.

"Oh, my beloved nephew and our distinguished Elder, what a great night this is!" she cried. She was still loud all right, but her words were so sweetly different. Elder Candy had been sweating from all the excitement and his sweaty hands began to lose grip of his Sacra Vellum. He stooped down to rescue it before it landed on the grass. Attitudah noticed. "Ah, your Sacra Vellum. Let's read together, Elder." Before Elder Candy had a chance to decide, she was at his side. "Open it, open it."

There was childlike excitement in her voice. "Let's see what Imortul is saying to us." Elder Candy held up the book for Attitudah and himself to view. He wouldn't spoil this treasured moment. TW managed to peer over. Illuminated before their eyes, were the words, "Be filled with joy."

With great gusto, Elder Candy let out a euphoric shout, "Yes! Yes! Yes! We will be filled with joy."

TW laughed aloud, cartwheeling a couple of times, and hardly containing himself. "Dad would be glad, Dad would be glad!" he chanted. Then, jumping up and down, he yelled with delight, "This joy is better than a thousand lollipops!"

"I like that!" chuckled Elder Candy heartily. His joyful voice bellowed through the midnight sky, "We've found a joy greater than a thousand lollipops!"

Almost in unison the children responded delightfully, "*Yeah! Yeah! Yeah!*"

14

"Come on, precious people. Let's head down the hill, back to Graceville, back to our homes. The hope of all generations has finally come," Elder Candy heartily ushered them homeward. There was much laughter, singing, and clapping. The Graceville Pollinators rushed forward to lead the way, as if protecting a priviledged crowd. Their plan was to charge through the Inspector-guarded entryway. Elder Candy smiled at their zeal, but he knew the Optima Dona would help, just as Messenger Joygive had promised. TW was still cartwheeling and acting wild with excitement. He spun around till he got dizzy, bumping left and right into equally-excited people. Then he bumped into Professor Smartee, revealing his brewing thoughts.

"Contain your foolery, young lad. No doubt this is a great experience for all of us, but we need to be thinking about some serious realities."

"And what realities could those be, Professor Smartee?" Elder Candy curiously asked with a raised eyebrow, protectively putting his arm around TW's shoulder. Those around them stopped their jubilation to listen. The inquiring calm seemed to usher Professor Smartee to share more of what was on his mind.

"The reality is that we are going to be hated and envied by those within the city. What quality of life would it be for us to live amongst those who hate us? We have been banished, and we will certainly not be welcomed by the Elders or the people." Then he raised his voice even louder, as if beckoning a larger audience. " I want to propose to Elder Candy and to all of you out here, that we all remain here on Lonely Hill and build a city for ourselves; a city of Sacra Vellum-readers. I can see it now—Sacraville! We will be the intellectual stimuli for the entire Monkonian region. As early as tomorrow, I can begin to put together building plans, starting with an institution of learning. This will be important to uncover deep secrets of the Sacra Vellum and research its great powers. We will be sought after by many for our wisdom and our…"

His speech was interrupted by an agreeing Grandma Selfyade, "We can begin with a tent city. I brought two tents with me tonight. I'll be willing to give up the second tent for some to share."

Mr. Hopelett jumped in saying, "That's very kind of you, Grandma Selfayde, but it is completely impractical. We have a crowd here, not one or two people."

"And besides, no one would want to share a tent with me. You have never heard an earth-shattering snore like mine!" another man joked.

"As I was saying…," continued Professor Smartee, visibly irritated. But he was interrupted yet again. This time it was Mr. Lorner who interjected.

"I just can't begin a new way of life from nothing. Let's not be theoretical here. I have a music recital to oversee tomorrow. I need to get back into Graceville."

"And I have floral deliveries for two weddings," added Attitudah.

"Would those be petal papyrus or real flowers?" taunted another. The buzz of debates, discussions, and responses had clearly begun to chip away at their joy. Elder Candy sensed that a new chapter of fearful commotion was about to begin. He quickly tried to recapture their focus.

"Imortul's vision was for Graceville, not just for a handful of us who came out tonight. We must take this joy to them, also. This was what we were commanded by

Messenger Joygive."

"That's great," Professor Smartee opposed again, "but what is the plan to get us in?" TW could still hear the Graceville Pollinators joyfully chanting freedom tunes in the distance, as they led the way, totally unaware of the brief interruption that had just occurred somewhere in the middle of their procession. He felt so energized by their joyful shouting that boldness stirred up within him. He was going to put on the bravery of one of those valiant generals in his imaginary army. He pulled himself away from Elder Candy, who was deeply engrossed in dousing all the exploding opinions, pulled off his shirt, and started waving it wildly in the air, right in the presence of the debating adults. He shouted at the top of his lungs, straining his vocal chords to be heard.

"We will not retreat! I raise the banner of the revealed Sacra Vellum, and I say, let's march forward into Graceville!" His words could not have been more arresting, forcing a hush on the arguing crowd.

"TW, was that really you?" questioned an impressed Elder Candy, breaking the stunned silence. "What incredible boldness and wisdom from a twelve-year old! You have undoubtedly grown beyond the comforts of lollipops. Citizens of Graceville, TW couldn't have said it better. We should not be ashamed to accept wisdom when we recognize it, even if it is from a young one." He looked around to all, affirming acceptance of TW's words,

"There'll be no more ideas or excuses. We must trust that the Optima Dona will help us." Attitudah, in quite an uncharacteristic manner, suddenly ran towards TW and wrapped her arms around him.

"Forgive me, TW," she cried, choking back a tear. "Even if I had shred every Sacra Vellum in existence, I could never have reached the one in your heart. You are truly your father's son."

Excerpt from The Graceville Chronicles Book Two

"...I'm sorry TW, I have to turn you in," she choked.

"Aunty, what did I do wrong? All of us who were at the hill, who enjoyed the first reading of the Sacra Vellum, promised to look out for each other. Why are you being a traitor, Aunty. I thought you had changed." TW was shaking his head in total disbelief. "Was he wrong to have trusted her?"

"TW, I am not turning you in because I am betraying our hill group...the Ekkleyzians, as we're now called. There's something I ought to have told you. Something that has caused me sleepless nights for many years..."

"What! what!..." His face was suddenly filled with terror and his heart was pounding loudly.

"Here. This is meant for you." Attitudah thrust a small clay pot into his trembling hands. He slowly opened it.

"What's this?" He grimaced at the black dust inside the small clay pot she had just handed him. His initials were even carved into its side.

"It's the story of your..."

Bang! Bang! Bang! Attitudah cringed.

"I'm sorry, they're here." She looked beyond TW's shoulder toward the door. The rage-filled Chief Townsitter was impatiently pacing back and forth at the doorway; Inspector Jaw was with him!

"Who's here?" TW asked in a strained whisper, too scared to turn around and look. "Tell me, what don't I know about myself..."

Acknowledgements

First of all, I bow my head in utmost gratitude to the Lord Jesus Christ for giving my life a new page on which He writes my life story. Not an obscure story which I may accidentally dabble in and out of, but a clear and certain story – filled with immeasurable grace and mercy. As author over my life, He titles each chapter and is intimately involved in every scene. Best still, he knows the glorious end of it – Me, being with Him! Knowing Christ has provided the inspiration for Light for the Sacra Vellum.

At the onset of this writing project, I was certainly not aware of how I'd be dependent on the resources of many to bring it to completion. I have come away with a fresh awareness of how immensely blessed I am, because God filled my life with generous individuals who gave of their resources to make it happen. I'd like to use this space to thank them all:

To my dear friend, Karen Hart – You've been with me on this project right from the start. Thank you for urging me to write this book. I'm not quite sure how you sustained enthusiasm for this project for over two years or how you were deaf to my most credible excuses for why I needed to keep putting it off. Everyone needs a friend and an accountability partner like you!

To my team of reviewers – Melody Caton, Shannon Woodruff, Joanna Breault, Bunmi Oloruntoba, Shannon Seaman, Toni Lynn Barto, Matt Terl, Joe King, and Will Manus. Thanks so much for generously giving of your time, insight, and encouragement. Matthew, Toni Lynn, and Will, how can I forget reading your numerous comments and sighing, "Wow, this is nothing short of a rewrite." And there were several rewrites! Thank you for your editorial expertise.

To my Youth review team across the States – Jesse Johnson, Adeyoola Adeniji, Benjamin Campbell, Courtney Flonta, Rachel Epp, and Christopher Aboagye. You kids gobbled up this book faster than I imagined you would, and then you asked for more…you've put fire in my bones! Thank you!!

To my editor, Emily Wright – Thanks for your enthusiasm and hard work.

To my proof readers, Lisa Epp and Elaine Dudley – Your input was exceptional. I am immensely blessed to have benefitted from your attention to detail. I couldn't say enough thank yous!

To my illustrator, Lisa Wright – It was so much more than your talent. It was your sweet spirit, your humility, and your total dependence upon God that made this such a beautiful sisterly experience. Thank you! Please enjoy the work of your hands.

To my mentor, Dr. Friday Bekee – Thanks for the several years of wonderful mentorship and fervent prayer support you provided me with. I know you'd be overjoyed to have this book in your hands.

To my many prayer partners – Your prayers were the back-bone of this project. Thank you for your faith-filled intercession.

To my dear family in the UK – My brother, Ben, my sister, Esohe, and my sister-in-law, Nana – Thanks for all your wonderful "back office" support and enthusiasm.

To my wonderful parents, Edward and Esther Iyamu – Thank you for your sacrificial love and your lavish investment in my education. Here's more fruit for you.

To my precious children – Toluwani, Reolu, and Oyinda. Finally, the "book on tape" can be read. Thanks for all those car trips where the only agenda was listening to me read aloud to you. You were a great sounding board. Boys, I had tons of fun just listening to you comment on plots, characters, and various illustrations. This was a long project for me but you kept it fresh.

To my darling husband, Toks – Thank you for dreaming along with me. You and our children keep me in constant awe of God's goodness.

About the Illustrator

Lisa Wright holds a Bachelors of Art degree in Fine Arts from Mount Holyoke College, Massachusetts, where she specialized in Studio Art and minored in Art History and French. She also studied Art in Paris during her Junior year, taking classes in Art History through the Wesleyan College European program and L'Ecole de Louvre. She studied drawing at L'Ecole des Beaux Arts while living in Paris.

Lisa has been drawing for as long as she can remember, but began exhibiting and selling her work while in high school, competing in local and regional art shows. Her work has received recognition through numerous "best of show" awards, including the Scholastic Art Award of Ohio several years in a row. Her commission work has included murals, drawings, and paintings. Samples are available for viewing at christianartclass.com. Light for the Sacra Vellum is the first book she has illustrated.

Lisa is married to Tim Wright and they make their home in Norfolk, Virginia where she has taught art, through a private program, for more than ten years while homeschooling their four children.

About the Author

Cathy Idowu holds an MBA from University of Illinois. She began her career providing business communications for systems analysts. A couple of years later, she transitioned into a technical writing career to provide her with the flexibility she needed as a working mom. After nine years of technical writing, she resigned her corporate work to devote more time to raising her young children. While at home, she has been able to make time to pursue her desire to write wholesome fantasy/ fiction.

Cathy began writing stories in 6th grade. At the time, she had a hand-written Enid Blyton-inspired adventure series, supplying eager classmates with a steady stream of fun reading. A couple of grades later, the "fun" was encroached upon and eventually swallowed up by a deluge of pre-college homework and additional extra-curricular activities. Cathy's passion for writing was refueled after she came to the knowledge of Christ, the Savior. Over the last twelve years she has written several christian-themed articles and short stories for a christian publication, as well as numerous skits for youth Sunday school use.

Cathy, and her husband, Toks Idowu, make their home in Virginia Beach, Virginia. They are blessed with two sons and a daughter.

www.gracevillechronicles.com

Printed in the United States
144337LV00003BB/11/P

9 780980 148404